Duck
Stories

Jenny Tyler and Philip Hawthorn
Illustrated by Stephen Cartwright

Consultant: Betty Root
Edited by Heather Amery

04272

Notes for Parents

This is a book to share with a young child who is beginning to talk. At this stage of their development, children need lots of opportunities to learn new words and phrases, and lots of practice using those they already know in different ways and situations. Each picture in this book is designed to stimulate discussion about what Duck is doing and about the things around him. There are objects to name and things to spot or count. The text on each page is intended only as a starting point for wider conversation.

Very young children have to learn that a book has a sequence and that, by starting at the beginning and turning the pages one by one, they can follow this sequence to find out what happens next. The pictures in this book tell three short, very simple stories for children who are just ready to learn this important new skill.

Duck
and his friends

Here's Duck who has a brand new hat,
He hears a rustle, up pops Cat.

They leap and jump and hop so high,
To try and catch a butterfly.

They're very hot, but help is near,
It's Frog who has a bright idea.

Both Duck and Frog enjoy a swim,
But Cat's not sure if she'll go in.

They want some lunch, but what to do?
Then peeping Piglet says, "Er ... Boo!"

He says, "Dig in, it's only swill,
I hope it doesn't make you ill."

Then Duck and Piglet, Frog and Cat
Find funny Monkey with Duck's hat.

And now the fun and games begin,
They all play ball games, guess who'll win.

"My tummy's rumbling now," croaks Frog,
"It must be time to eat," barks Dog.

They eat their picnic, food galore!
Then Piglet grunts and starts to snore.

His friends are hiding all about,
Duck needs your help to seek them out.
(So when you spot each one, just shout!)

Duck
on holiday

Here's Duck who thinks, this sunny day,
The beach is just the place to play.

This nice cool rock pool seems to be
The perfect Duck-sized bit of sea.

He steers his rubber ring with style,
And chats to Fish for quite a while.

Then sails his yacht, and calls with glee,
"Ahoy there, shipmates, look at me!"

Duck slurps a drink, gets nicely tanned,
And eats a sandwich on the sand.

He builds a castle, digs a moat,
Adds flags and shells, and then his boat.

The ball goes smash, poor Duck starts crying,
Shells go crash, and flags go flying.

Dog shares his nice ice cream with Duck,
To make up for his rotten luck.

The two new friends then scream and shout,
While whizzing round and round about.

It's time to go, Duck feels so sad,
He thinks of all the fun he's had.

It's hard to leave, but have no fear,
He'll see his friends again next year.

Duck
in trouble

Here's Duck, who hopes that very soon,
He'll have a big, fat, round balloon.

He starts to rise and holds on tight,
He looks just like a funny kite.

Atchoo! He sneezes, what a shame!
And falls back down to earth again.

He gives poor Bird a dreadful shock,
The nest begins to roll and rock.

The tree branch breaks and with a crack,
They both fall down and Duck says, "Quack!"

Where Duck before was green and scruffy,
Now he looks all clean and fluffy.

So Duck drips dry, but trouble's brewing,
Watch that cat, what is she doing?

As Duck goes splat, he hears a laugh,
Says Cat, "Enjoy your muddy bath!"

What's next for Duck, I do declare!
A bubble bath extraordinaire.

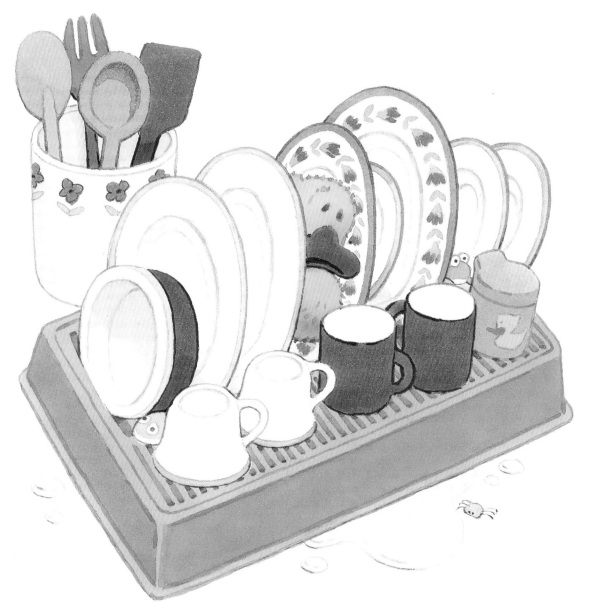

The soggy Duck now needs to dry,
He shakes his feathers with a sigh.

Duck goes to bed, he's tired out.
What do you think he dreams about?